Introduction

Join my newsletter for the latest info on new releases: https://subscribepage.io/Gkj4yZ

Contents

To breaking out of your shell.
Whatever that means for you.

Chapter 1

The elves are hard at work this Christmas season, their chatter filling the air with excitement and anticipation. They're racing against time to finish making all the toys for good girls and boys around the world. Every year has been like this since I've known him, which has been a very long time, and I don't see things changing any time soon.

While I'm immensely proud of my husband's occupation, I can't help but feel like I'm being left behind as Mrs Claus, watching from the sidelines while he spends far more time in his workshop than he does with me. It's been weeks since we've had a proper connection, and I'm growing increasingly frustrated.

It's hard to be mad at someone when they're going off to work each day providing for our family. I don't resent him for that one bit, and in fact I really appreciate and admire him for his dedication. But it's not like he goes onto a big box store website and clicks that he wants 500 of these and 1,200 of those. No, he painstakingly ensures that his elves make each gift to his exacting quality control standards.

Given the number of boys and girls in the world eligible for gifts, he runs a very streamlined staff. I've talked to him about automating, leveraging artificial intelligence, growing his team, but he has been resistant, insisting on doing things the 'traditional way.'

I respect his craft, but I really need him to get with the times if he wants this to work in the long-term. I'm not sure how many more holiday seasons I can take without employing drastic measures.

I get that the children deserve their toys, I really do. It's just that Mrs. Sissy Claus—that's me, by the way—has her needs, too, and the holidays can be a lonely time of year. Especially for me.

Chapter 2

"I know I tend to neglect you this time of year, Sissy dear," my husband sighs over dinner. He removes his gold-rimmed spectacles and keeps hold of them in his left hand as he lifts his gaze to meet mine.

"It weighs heavily on me every year, my love. It's so important that we give all the children the gifts they've worked so hard for all year, and I can't risk letting any of them down. But by being so good at my job, well, I'm afraid I've been letting *you* down. Neglecting my husbandly duties, sometimes for weeks at a time. That's not fair on you."

"I knew what I was signing up for way back then," I sigh. Unfortunately, I decided on a guy that everyone knew would be occupied for the months leading up to December, let alone the entire month itself being a massive inconvenience. It's not like he waited to spring it on me until after he got married.

Nope, Mr. Claus has been transparent about his work obligations the whole way through, proud of them even. It was me who decided not to listen, thought I knew better, could figure out a way for things to change. How naive.

But Mr. Claus is a good man, and I don't regret the choice I made to be with him for eternity or divorce, whichever comes first. Come January when we're on our annual refresher vacation after the busy season, I'll have long since shed these sentiments and be sunning myself with a good book on a lounger in the south of France.

"Well, nevertheless, you deserve better," he says. "And I've been thinking... we have a perfectly fantastic group of entertainers here amongst our elves. I don't take all of them with me when I'm working, and they have time to spare that they could be spending with you."

"Oh, yes, I suppose." I hadn't ever really thought of my husband's workers as a source of potential friendships. I'm not opposed to it or anything, they just always seem so happy and part of their own little clique.

"So," my husband presses forward, clearly with something more to tell me, "I've been talking with them and, well, we have an idea."

I'm touched, and more than a little guilty. Even with everything he has on his plate this time of year, he must really have noticed how miserable I've been.

"Whatever could you have in mind?'

"The elves have promised to take care of you while I'm off working... whatever that entails. To cater to your every whim. And I mean anything at all, it's yours. You just say the word and they'll do it."

I look at him from under my eyelashes. "You really mean *anything* goes?"

"Yes, anything at all. And honey, I know that you've been craving some good cock, any cock really. So that's very much on the table, too. You get yourself satisfied emotionally, spiritually, physically... sexually. This way, I'll get my work done and you'll be happy, so we'll all be happy."

"And you're... you're sure you're okay with this?"

He shrugs. "What choice do I have? And anyway, happy wife, happy life."

Okay, I think to myself. Why not? There's nothing left to lose, and everything to gain.

"When–when will this, uh... arrangement start?"

"As soon as I give them the word, my love. How does tomorrow sound?"

"That's soon, but it sounds perfect." I smile at him.

He smiles back at me, grasping my hand in his as he finishes his dessert.

What an interesting holiday season this is turning out to be.

Chapter 3

A spark of hope ignites within me when I hear Demanding Elf cough softly outside our door. It's a distinctive cough, a little husky, like he's chain smoked since coming out of the womb.

Out of all the elves. Demanding has always been rather forward with his advances. With him, there's no beating around the bush.

Although I've never crossed the line with him, I can tell by his style that he's rough and roughhousing, just what I'm craving. I slip off my fluffy red robe with white trim slowly, revealing my black lace lingerie underneath. It's not the most modest of outfits, but it makes me feel sexy and confident.

Demanding Elf pushes past the door without even knocking, his eyes falling instantly to my chest. "We're finally doing this then? It's taken you long enough." He looks around the room. "Sultry Elf isn't here yet?" he asks, licking his lips nervously.

"No, she isn't," I say with a smirk, taking a step closer. "But I am."

He swallows hard, his dark eyes darting down to my breasts and then back up to meet mine. "Well, then... I guess we'll have to make do," he murmurs. His hands are already on my hips, pulling me against his hardness as his fingers dig into my flesh. It's not a gentle touch, but I like it. I like it a lot.

I press myself against him, feeling his erection through our clothes. "You'd better be good to me," I whisper, lifting his elf shirt to reveal his well-defined pecs and circling his nipple with my tongue. His body shudders under my touch as I trace the line of his elf suit down to his belt buckle, undoing it quickly.

He groans and pushes me against the wall, pressing his hips against mine in a more intimate way than he's done before. "I'll be as good as you want me to be, Sissy Claus," he rasps, biting my bottom lip softly.

Sissy Claus. I still love the sound of my married name. I moan into his mouth before pulling away, tracing my tongue along his gently stubbled jawline. "We don't have much time," I say breathily, my voice shaking slightly with anticipation. "Show me what you've got." The truth is, we have time, and I intend on making the most of every minute of it.

Without wasting another moment, Demanding Elf spins me around, pinning me against the wall roughly, my face and breasts pressed up against the hard surface this time. His hand is at my thigh, pushing up my skirt slowly, and I gasp as his fingers brush against my panties. He smirks and growls, "You're wet," before plunging his finger inside me without warning.

I cry out, arching my back and digging my nails into the wall.

"Fuck," he mutters, kissing my neck wildly while fucking his finger in and out of me.

The room is spinning and I can hear the fire crackling in the fireplace, smell the vanilla scent from our cookies in the air as he continues pressing me hard into the wall.

"Harder," I whisper, pushing back against his hand.

Demanding Elf grunts and complies, adding another finger to surprise me. "You want this cock or these fingers?" he asks roughly, his free hand rubbing over his thick bulge as he presses it into the small of my back.

"Both," I manage to gasp out, my mind lost in the pleasure he's giving me. He chuckles darkly and kisses his way down my neck, trailing soft kisses and nipping at my skin delicately.

Sultry Elf appears in the doorway, looking bewildered but intrigued by what she sees–the rough passion between us that couldn't wait for her late arrival. She licks her lips as Demanding Elf continues to finger-fuck me, watching us intently. It's almost too much, it's hot.

She watches us with hooded eyes, biting her lip as she rubs herself through her panties. I can feel the heat emanating off her, her need for release evident. She's usually clothed in form-fitting gowns that showcase her ample cleavage and shapely hips, but tonight apparently underwear was her only temporary concern.

The fire pops, the whiskey is set aside, and in an instant, we're all on the bed and Shady Elf is straddling Demanding Elf's hips. She wears nothing but a tiny white thong, with crystal rhinestones, that leaves little to the imagination. Her pussy glistens with arousal, and her large breasts sway temptingly as she rides his cock slowly with her underwear still on. "Ready for company? Take what you want," she says with a wicked grin. She kisses her way down his body, leaning down to lap at the pre-cum on his erection. "Did you miss me?"

"Thank you, sexy," Demanding Elf murmurs, grabbing a handful of her hair and using his grip to pull her up so her face is inches from his. "And I always miss you, even when I'm inside your sweet pussy I'm missing the next time it's going to happen." He grabs her hips roughly and pulls her close so their lower halves touch. My pussy clenches as I remember what it felt like to grind my pussy against his skilled, calloused fingers just moments ago.

Next thing, Sultry hops off Demanding and she helps me onto him. And then his hands are on me. And then her hands are on me. And I lose all sense of who is doing what, all I know is that it feels very, very good.

We dance together like this, two Christmas elves and a human, and they take turns using my body as they please. I feel like I'm at the center of some twisted pornographic film as Demanding Elf thrusts into me while Sultry Elf grinds against my leg, her clit rubbing against my thigh. After what feels like hours of lovemaking, fluctuating from lazy and languid to frenzied and hardcore–mainly the latter, Shady Elf enters the room and watches, his hands clutching the mantle as he breathes heavily, his excitement clear.

The fire crackles, burning brightly as they take turns using me, their skilled fingers finding all my sweet spots, spurred on by the addition of a watcher. My mind is a blur of pleasure as I'm filled by both of them at once, their rough, demanding lovemaking everything I've ever wanted. Their scent of pine and cinnamon mixes with their musk, driving me wild.

"Oh fuck," I moan as Demanding Elf's clever tongue laps at my clit, sending waves upon waves of pleasure coursing through my body. Sultry Elf groans, burying her face in my neck as she too comes hard, her body shuddering against me, driven to release by the unrelenting vibrations on her clit. Shady Elf approaches us and leans down to lick up every drop of Sultry's juices, eyes glinting with lust. I can't turn away from the sight of his tongue working her pussy.

"You're so wet...so fucking wet," Demanding Elf murmurs against my skin, his voice rough with desire.

"Christmas just got a whole lot hotter," Sultry Elf pants out before climbing onto my lap, her plump ass on all fours, inviting Demanding Elf to take her while she's on top of me.

I sit still, watching Demanding feeling powerful and dominant as he slides into her tight heat. Dipping my head, I take one of her breasts in my mouth, suckling on her nipple and teasing it with my teeth. Shady watches us with a predatory gleam in his eyes.

"Merry fucking Christmas," Demanding and Sultry both whisper in unison, their hips moving in tandem as Demanding fills Sultry up completely.

Demanding pushes Sultry and I onto the bed next to each other, roughly yanking our thighs apart while we're side by side so we're both spreadeagled before him, our glistening pussies exposed for his viewing pleasure.

He lines up his impressive cock and thrusts it into me several times, causing me to cry out as his cock drags against my walls, and then sticks it into her, and then back into me. The bed squeaks beneath us as we grind together, creating a rhythm that matches the sound of the squeak.

I can't help but moan out loud as he takes us like this, their movements so expert that they could be choreographed. I feel used, and I've never been happier. Demanding's hand traces circles around my clit, adding just enough pressure to send me over the edge again, and I scream out his name.

"Claim what's yours," Sultry Elf demands, her breasts bouncing enticingly as she watches me come.

"Mine," I growl, moaning as Demanding thrusts deeper into us both. "Yours."

As we reach our climax together, sweat drips down our bodies, our skin sticky with each other's essence.

They collapse onto me, kissing and nibbling their way down my neck.

Shady joins us on the bed and spoons me from behind. I lean back into his hard body as his arms wrap around me.

"You're perfect for us," Shady Elf whispers in my ear, nuzzling closer.

"We're perfect for you," Sultry Elf adds, her breath hot against my skin.

Our hearts beat in unison as we catch our breath, completely spent.

Chapter 4

"Did you decorate the house?" Mr. Claus asks as he walks in, oblivious to what just happened between me, Demanding, Sultry and Shady. We're all sitting around the kitchen table having steaming cups of hot cocoa.

He removes his giant red coat and places it on a hook in the hallway, and then takes a seat at his desk which in December expands from a regular-sized computer desk and takes over the entire dining table.

I feel a stab of frustration but also relief that he's finally noticing some of my efforts. But I want him to see me like this—wanted and desired for my efforts *today*—not noticing something that took a month and was completed three weeks ago.

"Yes, I did, and it was finished about three weeks ago," I say slowly, fighting back the urge to roll my eyes as Demanding gives me a sympathetic glance. "Why do you ask?"

"Oh, it looks amazing," he replies quickly, looking around with wonder in his eyes before returning to the work on his desk.

I bite my bottom lip and watch as he focuses on work once again, his hands flying across the keyboard while visions of us together dance in my mind. It's like I'm not even here sometimes—like I don't exist in his world except as an accessory to make his life easier.

To cook, to clean, to keep the house in order. To remember to pay bills to keep the power and TV on–and wi-fi at the North Pole is no joke–to keep the sleigh maintenance current, and to keep everyone in good spirits, especially when he's off on one of his work trips.

But things need to change. There's an ache inside me that only he has ever been.able to satisfy–or perhaps I should clarify, that I've only ever let *him* satisfy–but he's not taking any steps to satisfy it, except for our earlier conversation which gives me hope he's finally taking notice–and it's growing stronger every day.

It's time to take matters into my own hands, to expedite things.

I saunter over to him, my hips swaying as the red dress hugs every curve. "Do you want some help with that, baby?" My voice is low and husky, tainted with the desire that hangs heavy between us.

He looks up, startled by my appearance but doesn't stop working. His erection is obvious through his pants and it takes everything in me not to crawl over his desk and take care of it right then and there. He shifts in his seat and glances at his mountain of paperwork and then back to me, guilt riddling his face. He's torn, conflicted, and I know who or what will ultimately win. "Oh no, darling," he says almost absentmindedly. "I've got this."

I want to scream but instead, I walk back to the kitchen, trying to ignore the ache that's building between my legs. Mr. Claus may not care, but I do. I was already developing an appetite, but the elves only made me more hungry with their touch and their demands.

Still, I'm not one to give up and I decide to give him one more chance to be the one to give me what I need. I cook his favorite meal slowly, four courses,, taking extra care with each dish, hoping he'll notice the effort. The smell of garlic and onions fills the air, making my mouth water uncontrollably.

By the time he finally looks up from his work again, I'm standing by his side with a glass of wine and an expression that says 'I'm all yours.'

We eat our meal, Mr. Claus deep in thought. "This is nice," he says absentmindedly. 'Nice' is a macaroni cheese TV dinner. Nice is a Salisbury steak that can be swallowed without needing to chew every bite for 90 seconds. What I made was a masterpiece, and he's giving me a 'nice'?

How was your day?" I ask, attempting to get past his careless choice of words.

"Fine," he responds absentmindedly while he flicks through his phone. "How was yours?"

"Oh, you know. Had a three-way with two hot elves while a third one watched. They gave me more pleasure in a few hours than you have tried to in the past few years, and we're planning a repeat sometime soon."

"That's nice dear," says my husband, continuing to scroll through his phone. I know he doesn't listen to everything I say–in fact, he makes jokes about it–but this is surely something that should have gotten his attention.

Maybe we've lost our spark.

Maybe this is it for us.

Just as well I have a few new friends to keep me company...

As I lay in bed, my husband, Mr. Claus, kisses my cheek and whispers, "I love you," before disappearing out the door. He's off on his final test run before his annual trip around the world to deliver presents, leaving me here alone in the North Pole with only his elves for company.

There's a knock on my door before Sultry Ass comes breezing through my room.. Her plump ass sways enticingly as she walks in, dressed in a form-fitting gown that shows off her ample cleavage and shapely hips. Her hair falls over one eye seductively, and she smiles at me, licking her full lips.

"We have a surprise for you, Mrs. Claus," she says, her voice husky.

Surprise... huh? I frown, not really sure what to expect but curious all the same.

The next thing I know, Sultry Elf is leading me to a dimly lit room where the other four elves are waiting. They all bow their heads respectfully as I enter, their eyes full of mischief. And then everything goes blurry because suddenly, they're all over me.

Their hands are like magic, running down my arms, my legs, and along my sides. The touch is feather-light, but their intentions are anything but gentle. I gasp when cool oil is rubbed onto my skin, and then it gets even better when they start massaging every inch of my body with expert hands that know just where to go.

"You like that, Sissy?" whispers Sulty Elf in my ear, her breath warm against my neck. "Tell us what you want."

Her voice sends shivers down my spine, and I don't even try to suppress the moans that escape when their hands find my tingling skin. Their fingers dig into my flesh just right, kneading out the tension from my muscles while their hot breath skims across my skin. I can't believe this is happening, but I don't want to fight it anymore.

"Oh God, don't stop," I breathe out, arching into their touch.

Delighted by my response, they move in sync, their hands running up and down my body in perfect harmony. They work together to undress me slowly, their eyes hungrily devouring every inch of my skin as it's revealed. Their touch is electric as they caress every curve and grope every luscious part of me.

This massage turns into so much more when they kneel around me and start kissing their way down my thighs, taking their time to tease my sensitive flesh with their lips and tongues. I'm lost in a haze of pleasure as their lips brush over my pussy, their hot breaths fanning across my folds.

Razor Elf looks up at me with hooded eyes before dipping his head again to take a taste of my nectar. "Mmm, she's so sweet," he murmurs, his tongue and its piercing both teasing my clit while the others continue their assault on my body with their hands.

I can feel the wetness coating his lips as he sucks on it, sending shockwaves of pleasure coursing through my core.

His fingers slip inside me, stretching my tight opening as another elf grips my aching nipples, rolling them between his fingers.

"More," I plead, my voice hoarse with need. I need this, need them, need more of their touches and attention.

Sex God Elf clasps his hands on my hips and guides my ass towards his face, his warm breath caressing my entrance. His tongue darts out, tracing the sensitive skin around my entrance before pushing inside me, making me gasp at the unexpected intrusion. He laps it up greedily as if he's been denied food for days.

The other elves join in, too, using their fingers to stroke and massage every inch of my pussy while their mouths devour me. My body quakes with each lick, each groan echoing in the dimly lit room.

"That's it, Sissy," Sultry Elf's voice whispers in my ear. "Give us your body, let us pleasure you."

I'm powerless against their onslaught; I can barely concentrate on breathing as they work in perfect unison to bring me to a screaming orgasm. My hips buck against their faces as they take turns licking and sucking until finally, all of me catches fire, and I come undone in their loving hands and mouths.

"Yes," I cry out, biting my lip to stifle my moans.

Tricky Elf slides in next, the steel bar from his pierced cock rubbing against my slick folds before he thrusts deep inside me, making me yell out in surprise but also in pleasure.

He starts to pump harder and faster, hitting that spot inside me that sends shockwaves of sensation through my entire body.

His hips smack against my tingling clit with each downstroke, and the sound echoes in the quiet room as we fuck like wild animals.

Demanding Elf grabs my breasts roughly, pinching my hardened nipples while he watches us intently.

"Oh God, they're good," I hear him mutter under his breath.

As if on cue, the other elves move away, leaving Sultry Elf to wrap her plump lips around my throbbing clit as Shady pours whiskey on it. The warm liquid trickles down my slit, and she licks it all up, her tongue swirling around until I'm writhing in ecstasy.

Her piercing glances meet mine as she takes my clit deeper in her mouth. I know she's going to make me come again from the taste and feel of the booze and the magic being worked by her expert tongue.

"Drink this," Demanding Elf demands between rough kisses on my thighs, pointing at Tricky Elf's rock-hard cock.

I do as he says. I drink him—the taste of his cum mixed with the whiskey, my tongue lapping at his essence as if it's the last drop of water in the desert. My mouth pulses around Tricky Elf's cock, milking him for everything he has, and he gives it to me with one final powerful thrust before crying out his release.

Sultry Elf smirks at me, her chest heaving with exertion from witnessing and participating this frenzy. She stands up gracefully and saunters to the other side of the room, where she starts to undress slowly. Her voluptuous curves seem to beckon us over, and my mouth waters for more.

I watch, enraptured as Sultry Elf slips out of her form-fitting gown, revealing nothing but lacy black lingerie that doesn't hide her large breasts or shaved pussy. The other elves can't take their eyes off her, either.

She whispers something to the others, who nod in agreement before they head toward a small table piled high with toys. Sultry Elf looks at me coyly and motions for me to join them.

"But... what about Mr. Claus?" I manage to croak out, but no one answers—they're too engrossed in choosing their playthings.

Shady Elf grins wickedly, climbing on top of me again. This time he rubs harder, and I bite my lip at the feeling of his rough hands on my sensitive skin. His eyeliner smudges as he leans down to kiss me again, his stubble prickling against my neck.

"I'll take care of you, darling," purrs Sultry Elf, twirling a long piece of red rope suggestively. "In fact, Mr. Claus demanded it."

Tricky Elf appears in front of me next, eyes wild with excitement. His bright pink hair stands out even more against his dark skin as he dives right in, grabbing my hips roughly and thrusting his hips against me, his cock sliding straight into me without any further attempt at foreplay. Which is good, because all I want right now is cock. His to start with.

"Fuck, yeah," he breathes heavily, his pierced cock dragging along my burning walls. "You like that, you sexy cunt?"

I nod frantically, unable to speak around the feeling of fullness and pleasure coursing through me. He grins, his eyes alight with fervor, and starts to jackhammer me mercilessly—harder than anything I've ever experienced before as the others look on.

Every thrust sends shivers down my spine, making every nerve ending tingle and sing. Sweat drips from our bodies onto the leather chair beneath us, mixing together as we grind and moan and pray for release.

But then Razor Elf appears, holding a flickknife with a wicked gleam in his eyes. He walks around us, circling like a predator stalking its prey. My heart races as he approaches, and I tense up instinctively.

"Hop off," he motions to Tricky Elf to climb off me, and he does, slowly pulling his massive cock out of my cunt, allowing the metal bar to drag against me on its way out

"Don't worry, love," Sultry Elf coos, running a finger down my sweaty back. "He'll take good care of you."

Razor Elf chuckles darkly as he grabs my leg and slides the knife slowly up my thigh—it trails across my skin, making me shudder involuntarily. Next thing I know, we're on the floor, me spread out beneath him. His rough hands grip my thighs tightly, holding me open for his pleasure.

"You like pain, don't you?" He asks, his voice low and husky.

I nod dumbly, too caught up in anticipation to speak. He smirks, then grabs my thigh and slices into it—a thin line of blood trickles down my skin. I gasp but it doesn't hurt as much as it should; instead, it feels like an electric shock racing through my veins. He watches my reaction with hooded eyes, his fingers tracing the wound slowly while his free hand cups my breast roughly.

He reaches down to his own thigh and I gasp as he slices a line into his own skin, blood taking a moment before it pools at the entrance of the wound and then begins trickling out like mine. He dips his finger into his wound, covering it in a deep, sticky scarlet.

"Now taste," he commands, pressing his fingers to my lips. "Drink my blood."

I do as I'm told, licking up the sweet metallic taste from his fingertips cautiously. He grunts in approval, sliding one finger down to my quivering pussy, then another, spreading my wetness around. He pushes them inside me and my body shudders at the unexpected intrusion. It feels so fucking good to have his big strong fingers inside of me.

"That's it, baby," he growls, thrusting his hips forward so his cock glides against my entrance teasingly. "Get ready for me."

Before I can react, he slaps my ass hard and slams into me with a groan of satisfaction. His hips grind against mine, his cock sliding in and out of me almost lazily at first before picking up speed. He's a beast in bed—rough and demanding yet surprisingly tender. And I can't help but love every second of it as we move together under the mistletoe.

"I can't believe we're doing this on Christmas week!."

"Neither can I," he pants, his eyes locking onto mine as he kisses me again. "But it feels right. So let's keep going."

I nod. He makes good sense.

I bite my lip and arch my back, moaning as he hits that spot inside me that makes me see stars. His pace quickens, and his mouth trails to my neck where he bites gently before sucking a hickey into my skin.

He's claiming me, making it known he's had me, but he's one of several under this roof that can now say that, hickey or not.

The room spins around us, lost in a haze of lust and desire as we move together like two animals who've been starved for each other's touch for far too long. The others look on, fixated at the way our bodies rut against each other, primal, aggressive. We all know this won't last forever, but right now in this moment, all that matters is our need for one another.

We make love on the floor under the mistletoe, our clothes scattered around us as if they were never important to begin with. And when he comes inside me, I feel a shiver run through my whole body, my walls gripping him tightly as he groans into my neck. I can taste it as he fills my mashes his mouth to mine—hot, salty, and more than a little bittersweet.

Panting heavily, I glance over at Sultry Elf who smirks at me from across the room where she's still standing naked, watching our every move. Her large breasts sway enticingly as she approaches, her eyes dark and full of lust.

"Your turn," she says huskily, voice rough from arousal.

She towers over me, her fingers trailing down my body slowly as I watch through heavy-lidded eyes that betray just how much I want her. Her touch is feather-light on my skin, sending shivers down my spine as she trails them along my stomach and down to my pussy. I shudder when she finally strokes my clit, and my hips buck up off the floor in response. "I–I haven't been with many women before…"

"You're such a dirty girl," she chuckles darkly, leaning in to lick me. "And you say that, but you're a natural."

Her tongue is rough and demanding, teasing my opening before delving deeper, and I can't help but moan loudly. Her fingers find their way inside me too, stretching me open for her while her mouth devours every inch of my swollen flesh. It feels so good to be taken by another woman; it's an experience I never thought I'd have but one that I crave now more than ever.

I gasp as she sucks harder on my clit and thrusts her fingers deeper, hitting that spot inside me that makes me see stars. And then she pulls away, leaving me shuddering and begging for more. She stands up, eyes glinting with mischief as her naked form glows under the soft overhead light, showcasing her angles and curves and making my pussy clench even harder.

"Now it's my turn," she purrs, straddling my head.

I open my mouth eagerly, eager to taste her. Her pussy smells intoxicating, like roses and sin, and I suck eagerly at her folds as she lower herself onto my face. I don't care that I might not be doing it right—all that matters is the feel of her wet heat against my tongue and the way she gasps and moans as I tease her with my lips and tongue.

The fire crackles between us, and we both lose ourselves in our erotic dance.

As she rides my face, I can feel the bed shaking beneath us, and I know that the other elves are getting off watching us. Their breaths are ragged, and their hands are moving faster against their crotches. It only turns me on more. When she comes, her juices flood my mouth, sweet and delicious, making me want to taste more.

"Now it's your turn," she whispers to Demanding Elf, pulling me up from the bed roughly but gently.

I gasp as I watch her guide his fat cock into her pussy. "She's so tight, it's almost painful in the best possible way," he growls. His hips meet hers instinctively, driving deeper. He groans as they begin to move together, lost in the rhythm of their bodies colliding.

The room is hazy with the scent of arousal and sweat now, making the air feel thick around us. The fire crackles and pops, casting an orange glow against her pale skin as she grinds against him—her breasts smacking against his chest in time with their hips.

Shady Elf grabs a bottle of whiskey from somewhere and pours it all over my body, letting the amber liquid run over me before licking it off seductively, paying special attention to my nipples and belly button. I cry out as he goes lower, trailing his tongue along my slit before finally taking me into his mouth and swallowing me whole.

I watch in awe as he worships me, my eyes locked on his bobbing head and the way he devours me like I'm the most delicious meal he's ever had.

Sinzy Elf removes his designer T-shirt revealing that he too has a perfectly sculpted body, proud cock at the ready.

"Get on your hands and knees," he commands.

"Take it all," he commands, spreading lube onto his hands as he works his large fingers into my ass, starting with one and working his way up to three. The burn is intense but incredible as he stretches me open for him.

I gasp around a moan when he finally slides his cock in, feeling him fill me up from behind. It's bigger than I could have ever imagined, but

I want it all—every inch of him inside me. We begin to move together in time with the others, creating a rhythm of our own as our bodies slide and grind together in unison.

Sex God Elf, with nothing but a Santa hat still on, watches us in awe. His jaw clenches when he sees how much we both need this—how much we crave each other. His eyes trace over every inch of our entwined bodies before he slowly undresses himself, revealing his massive cock that juts out towards us.

I'm about to ask what he wants when Sultry Elf grabs my arm roughly, moving me to the side. Sinzy moves with me with his cock still inside. She never takes her eyes off Sex God Elf as he lays next ot us on the bed, and she begins to ride his impressive length while Sinzy Elf continues to fuck me from behind.

Our moans and grunts fill the air as we become one entity, creating a symphony of lust and desire.

We climax together, our bodies shaking violently, the room echoing with pleasure. As our cries die down, Sex God Elf joins us, coming on my stomach and chest from underneath Sultry.

The six of us lay in a sweaty tangle of limbs and desire, catching our breaths as we stare into each other's eyes.

This is the most perfect orgy I've ever been a part of.

Chapter 5

The next day, I wake up glowing like a Christmas tree, my body humming from the pleasures of last night. I can't help but smile as I recall the adventure with the four rowdy elves.

My mind wanders to how rough and sexy Shady Elf looked as he poured whiskey all over his naked body and demanded I lick it off after he did the same to me, my tongue flicking over every inch of skin before reaching his hard cock. I shudder with desire just thinking about it.

Then there was Demanding Elf, with his strict demeanor and delicious ass, pushing me into positions that made me scream with pleasure.

But it's Sultry Elf who takes up most of my thoughts. Her beautiful breasts bouncing as she rode Demanding, her eyes full of unadulterated lust as she ground herself against my pussy, as she lapped against my clit with her expert tongue.

I walk into the great hall where Mr. Claus is sipping on some hot cocoa, looking tired. "Morning, sir," I say, trying to keep my voice light. "Did you sleep well?"

He nods, but he doesn't look convinced. "Not as well as you, I see." He raises an eyebrow at me playfully.

"Well, I had a lot of fun last night," I admit with a blush.

"I'm glad for you, Sissy," he says with a soft smile. "But you know I'm not one for such... rowdy activities."

I nod in agreement, but I also know there's more to it than that . "You could give it a try, at least," I suggest softly. "The Elves really are a lot of fun, just like you promised. I know you haven't explored much with guys. So what about starting off with Sultry Elf? She's gorgeous, super hot naked, and has been dying for you to notice her."

He chuckles. "She's not the only one, my dear. But I'm not sure..." He trails off, looking unsure.

"Trust me," I say, my voice low and sultry like Sultry Elf herself. "You won't regret it."

He looks at me for a moment longer, considering my words. "Alright," he finally says, his voice barely above a whisper. "Tonight then."

I can't help but moan in anticipation. Tonight I'll get to watch Mr. Claus be pinned under Sultry Elf, just like she did to me, her plump ass bouncing as she takes my husband deep inside of her. Shady Elf will hold my hand while we watch, his eyes full of lust and whiskey-fueled desire. I shiver at the thought of it all.

The day drags on, but finally, it's time for Sultry Elf's night with Mr. Claus. She walks in a circle around him, dressed in her finest attire, trailing a finger over his broad chest and back as she makes her radius around his body. Sultry Elf wears a form-fitting gown that hugs her voluptuous curves, accentuating her cleavage and shapely hips.

Mr. Claus doesn't try to hide his desire as his eyes trail over Sultry's hot body. I'd be jealous but I'm just as turned on, especially knowing about her expert tongue and her tight hot cunt.

Demanding Elf dons an elegant suit, complete with a custom-made pocket square that matches his cold demeanor.

Shady Elf is shirtless, showing off his well-toned abs and piercings, his whiskey glass clinking against the ice in his hand.

Razor leans against a wall, opening and closing his flickknife as he waits for the action to commence.

The clock strikes midnight, and we all jump as it chimes through the air. The magic of Christmas fills the room, enveloping us all. The air is thick with lust and desire. "Well, I've heard so much about this from Sissy. Let's begin," Mr. Claus says with a wicked smile on his face.

Sultry Elf leads the way upstairs, pulling Mr. Claus by the hand behind her. Demanding Elf following close behind them, his heart racing in his chest. Shady Elf brings up the rear, licking his lips and trailing fiery fingers along the wall as they ascend. I stay back with Razor for a moment, watching them go, my panties already damp at the thought of what's to come.

Inside our chambers, Sultry Elf turns around slowly, casting a seductive glance over her shoulder at Mr. Claus. She closes the door behind her and locks it, trapping them in together. I hear soft giggles followed by the rustle of fabric as she begins undressing him slowly, her breath brushing against his skin as she reveals each inch of flesh.

Just as I start to get uncomfortable with the door standing between me and my husband and his hot little slut, the door clanks open, "Just kidding," she giggles. "It's way more fun if you watch." We enter the room and take our places on seats along one wall.

Demanding Elf watches intently as Sultry Elf peels off layer after layer of clothing until Mr. Claus stands before them both naked except for his red fluffy slippers. He's round but he's hot, his girthy cock springing to attention at the sight of Sultry Elf's curvy hips and the pleasure she's made it very clear she intends to give him tonight.

His cock further stiffens under her gaze, an impressive sight even to someone like me who sees far more than I should. Sultry Elf moans as she takes it into her hand, stroking it gently before taking it into her mouth, sucking on it like a lollipop while Demanding Elf watches on with hooded eyes.

I catch my breath at the sight of her head bobbing up and down on my husband's shaft, her tongue swirling around the tip teasingly as she looks up at him between strokes. I know what my husband's cock feels like in my mouth, it's glorious, and I'm excited to be sharing the same experience with Sultry Elf.

Demanding Elf leans in close, whispering something into Sultry Elf's ear that makes her giggle before she stands up straight again. She saunters towards me, her hips swaying enticingly, and I struggle not to touch myself as she runs her fingers lightly over the strap of my panties. "Sissy Claus," she says with a sultry purr, "it's time we get you ready for tonight's festivities."

I nod eagerly, taking deep breaths as she pushes me towards the bed. My heart races as I climb under the covers, wondering what she has in store for me.

As if reading my mind, she smirks wickedly and produces a bottle of whiskey from somewhere, pouring it generously all over my body. The liquid drips down my skin, warm and smooth against my chilled flesh. I don't know where they get their endless supply of whiskey, or why they enjoy pouring it on their and my naked bodies so much, but it works for me.

She wastes no time licking it off of me, her tongue tracing every curve and dip as if mapping out where she wants to taste next.

"Mmm," she hums as she reaches between my legs, dipping two fingers into my wetness and circling them around my entrance. I bite my lip at the sensation, surprised by how good it feels even after so many encounters with the Shady and Demanding and Razor and Sex God Elf.

When she slides them inside me, my walls clench around them greedily, demanding more. Sultry Elf's lips curl into a smile as she adds another finger, stretching me carefully.

Shady Elf steps closer, his eyeliner smudged from excitement as he watches her work.

My breath catches when Sultry Elf takes her fingers out and replaces them with her warm, wet mouth. She sucks on them before slowly sliding them back into place, working me with three fingers now.

I can't help but moan as she starts to move them in and out, her lips forming a perfect 'O' around them.

"You're so tight, baby," she whispers against my skin, kissing up my torso. "I can't wait to watch Shady Elf fuck you."

Her words send a shiver down my spine that has nothing to do with fear or uncertainty. The thought of watching Shady Elf take me sends waves of excitement coursing through me. "You want him to...?"

Sultry Elf nods, her fingers never stopping their rhythm as she answers. "I want you both. Together."

The image flashes through my mind, and I feel myself growing even wetter for them. "Yes, Sultry Elf. Anything you want."

She pulls her fingers out, leaving me aching and wanting more, and stands up. Her nimble fingers work at untying me, and soon enough, I'm free. She helps me to my feet and leads me over to a massive bed covered in red and green satin sheets. "On your knees," she demands softly, her voice thick with desire.

I comply without question, kneeling on the plush comforter. She positions me just right before stepping back, revealing a sight so erotic that I nearly come on the spot.

Sultry Elf's naked body glistens with her own arousal. My eyes wander over every inch of her, drinking in the sight of her full breasts and shaved pussy. My mouth waters at the thought of tasting them both. I watch my husband's eyes greedy with lust as they trail over her insanely hot body.

"Tell me what you want," she orders, her voice rough and low.

"I want you both," I whisper, glancing over at Shady Elf who nods in agreement.

Sultry Elf straddles me, her plump ass cheeks swaying as she lowers herself onto my face. I reach up to grope them, feeling how wet she is already.

She smells like warmth and woman and Christmas spirit. Her pussy is tangy and salty from her earlier pleasure, and I lap at it greedily, tonguing her clit while finger-fucking her entrance.

She gasps and moans above me, her hands in my hair urging me on.

Shady Elf kneels beside us, pouring whiskey all over himself before rubbing it over his cock.

He's hard as a rock already, leaking pre-cum onto the floor. He leans down and licks it up, tasting it before pouring more on himself.

My eyes follow as he drizzles the amber liquid over Sultry Elf's perfect breasts, watching him trace circles around her nipples with his tongue. She arches into the touch, pushing herself even deeper onto my face.

He grabs a handful of my hair, pulling me up roughly. "Your turn," he growls before shoving my head between his legs.

I take him in my mouth eagerly, taste him for the first time - he's musky and sweet like rum-soaked fruitcake.

My tongue swirls around his shaft, and I take more of him in, loving the feel of his thick length in my mouth. He groans deeply, thrusting into me as I suck him off.

Sultry Elf rocks her hips, grinding her pussy onto my face as Shady Elf and I swap flavors. I can feel his fingers tracing along my spine, sending shivers down my back. The room is hot and heavy with the scent of desire and whiskey.

Then, suddenly, it's all happening at once. Shady Elf pours the rest of the bottle over Sultry Elf, letting it drip down her body like honey. She moans as he begins to lick it off her, his long, wet tongue tracing her curves.

My tongue traces circles around the head of his cock, teasing him as he watches intently.

I take him deep into my mouth again, feeling him twitch in anticipation.

Glancing to the side, I see Mr. Claus, cock in hand, brow furrowed in intense concentration as he soaks in the sexy scene playing out before him.

Sultry cries out sharply when Shady flicks his tongue around her nipple and then laps at her wet pussy, licking up the whiskey that collects there. I can hear the sloppy sounds of their pleasure as they explore each other.

My mouth is filled with the taste of Shady when he yanks on my hair again. "Wrap your lips around me," he demands, thrusting his hips forward. I do as he asks, taking him deeper into my throat as their moans fill the room. The room spins around me in a haze of lust and lustful intent.

He pulls out roughly, coating my cheek with more pre-cum before sitting back on his heels. His hands grip my head tightly as he slams back into my mouth, his hips grinding against my face. I can almost taste the whiskey on his skin as he comes, filling my mouth with his hot seed. I swallow greedily, wanting more.

Desperate for release myself, I crawl up the bed to find Demanding Elf's cock, already leaking pre-cum onto the plush duvet. I take him into my mouth too, sucking hard on the shaft as though it's a lifeline.

The whiskey burns going down but I don't care as I feel his steady rhythm quicken beneath my lips.

It's not long before he groans, his hips bucking wildly as he unloads into my mouth. The bitter taste of the alcohol mixes with his seed but doesn't deter me from swallowing every drop. His hands grip my head tightly, holding me in place as he empties himself into me.

Shady Elf joins us, crawling over to where we lie entwined together. He dips a finger into the pool of whiskey on the sheets and then brings it to my wet pussy, circling it around my entrance teasingly. "Ready for more?" He winks, and before I can answer he slips inside me.

Heat ripples through me at his intrusion, making me gasp and arch my back off the mattress. Shady Elf starts to fuck me slowly, using the alcohol as lube. I can smell the sharp scent of it mixed with our sweat as he picks up pace, slamming into me hard.

"Oh fuck, Shady. Fuck me," I pant between their slurping noises and grunts. He kisses my neck, nipping at it gently before reaching for the bottle of whiskey again. I watch as he pours it over his cock, and when he pushes back inside me, the burn is intense but thrilling.

"Our very own Sissy Claus," he groans, thrusting faster now. "You're so tight. So wet. I can't get enough of you."

This is Christmas like I've never known it before–wild, passionate, and spicy. The scent of whiskey and sex fills the air, and I don't want it to end. Our pleasure-filled moans fill the empty room, echoing off the stone walls as we reach our climaxes together.

As I catch my breath, Sex God Elf enters the room, his eyes traveling over our entwined forms. He's topless as usual, just a towel wrapped around his shoulders and another around his hips, emphasizing his broad shoulders and narrow waist. His eyes gleam with curiosity and lust. "Ho, ho, ho," he chuckles, his voice deep and demanding. "Sultry and Sissy seem to be enjoying themselves quite well."

I look up at him, my cheeks flushed with arousal and satisfaction. As much as I love being dominated by Shady, I can't resist the allure of Sex God Elf, either.

Sultry Elf yanks Mr. Claus over to the bed roughly, rolling him onto his back with a smirk. She straddles him in one swift motion, her ample breasts bouncing enticingly as her pussy grinds down on his hard cock without her letting him enter her yet. He glances over at me as if for approval, and I just smile.

"What do you want, Sex God?" She grinds her hips down on Mr. Claus' cock teasingly, but her eyes never leave Sex God's face.

"I want what I've wanted since the moment I saw you," he growls. His hands move to her ass, squeezing the soft flesh with possessive force. "I want you to ride me, Sultry."

Without another word, Sultry jumps off my husband and moves over to Sex God She sinks down onto his shaft, taking him deep inside her. Her moans are louder than our previous ones combined as she begins to ride him hard and fast.

I watch them together; admiring how she's always been the best at pleasing men. I'm mesmerized by the way her pussy bounces up and down on Sex God's massive shaft.

Shivering, I move over to Mr. Claus and get him to get on his hands and knees. From behind him, I lean forward to lick around his asshole. He moans as I feel its heat and musk against my tongue. I trail kisses down his thighs, breathing in his musky scent–a mix of sweat, leather, and sex.

My cock throbs in anticipation at the thought of feeling him inside me. I press my head against the bed, hands clenching the fabric of the sheets desperately.

Sultry grinds her hips harder, meeting Sex God Elf's thrusts with precision. Her breasts bounce enticingly with each movement, the sound of skin slapping against skin echoing through the room. "Oh fuck," she moans, "Yes, fuck me harder, Sex God."

Somehow, Sex God Elf's hand finds its way to my mouth, his fingers tangling in my hair..

His hips jerk forward and his cock slides out of Sultry's wet pussy, only to plunge back in deeper. She cries out, arching her back as she takes him all in. Her body shakes with pleasure as they couple moves together in an erotic rhythm.

"You're so fucking beautiful, the both of you," he gasps. He pulls Sultry off him, leaving his erect, engorged cock pointing directly at me. His free hand grips my head and yanks it down into his lap, holding it in place as he begins to cum, filling my mouth with thick, salty nectar. I swallow every drop greedily, feeling the warmth spread through me as I taste the combination of Sex God and Sultry's arousal.

"I love the way you taste," I manage between mouthfuls.

"We love how you taste, too," Sultry whispers before leaning down and giving Sex God Elf's cock a cleansing lick of her own.

For the rest of the morning we find our balance, our pace, and fuck until morning light filters through the curtains, washing over us in a warm golden glow. Finally spent, we collapse in each other's arms, sweaty and sticky with lust. The scent of sex lingers in the air, mingling with that of pine needles and freshly baked cookies from the Christmas tree nearby.

Chapter 6

I can't help but giggle with excitement as I hurry to set the table, eager for Mr. Claus's arrival. The anticipation is driving me mad! I've missed him so much during his travels, and the thought of being bad and teasing him tonight fills me with delicious excitement. The air crackles with anticipation as I arrange cutlery and place the steaming bowls of vegetable soup in front of each place setting, my heart hammering in my chest like a reindeer on a frozen lake.

The door creaks open, and there he is, Santa Claus himself. His gaze trails over me, my body clad only in a ruffled apron and the insanely high heels that make his mouth water. He winks at me before striding over to the table, the jingle of his belt announcing his approach. My eyes dart down to the bulge in his pants as he leans over to kiss my cheek—it's always so big this time of year!

"Hey Santa? I've got your milk and cookies right here, and I've been a bad, bad girl," I whisper in his ear, and he shivers at the warmth of my breath on his neck.

As we sit down together, I can barely contain my excitement. The moment he sinks into his seat, I lean over to take his huge cock out of his pants, freeing it from its confinement. It springs out with a soft thwap sound that echoes through the room, a twinkling light in my eyes.

"Mmm...," I moan around a mouthful of food, licking my lips as I watch him dive into his meal. "You've been such a bad boy this season, Mr. Claus," I tease, my voice low and seductive. "I thought we could use some company again tonight."

Sultry Elf chuckles as she walks over and takes a seat beside me, her breasts bouncing under her tight gown as she nudges her plate towards him. She winks at me knowingly, clearly eager for us to get down to business while we eat.

We don't even make it through dinner before Mr. Claus is up around the table, tearing off my apron in one swift motion. His hands are rough but gentle on my skin as he pulls me close, his lips tracing a trail down my neck towards the small of my back.

My breath hitches when he licks across a patch of hot wax Razor Elf had applied earlier—damn that elf for being so inventive!—and then he's pushing me over the table, lifting one leg over his shoulder with surprising strength. I can feel his beard tickling my thighs as he buries his face between them, inhaling deeply as if drinking me in.

"Oh God," I gasp, arching into his touch as he licks and nibbles at my wet folds. Sultry Elf leans in close, nipples hard against her gown, her voice low and husky when she asks, "Does he please you, Mrs. Claus?"

"Yes," I moan, gripping the edge of the table tightly. "So much." Mr. Claus lifts his head from between my legs long enough to capture my mouth in a heated kiss, his tongue dancing with mine as he slowly but firmly pushes two fingers inside me.

"Ho ho ho," he chuckles, his voice rough with lust. "I think we'll be extra naughty this year."

Shady Elf steps forward, pouring him a shot of whiskey from a crystal decanter. He takes it and downs it in one gulp before walking over to us, his eyes locked on where Mr. Claus is pleasuring me. He leans down and whispers something in Sultry Elf's ear, making her giggle like a schoolgirl while she cups her own breasts, her nipples standing at attention under her sheer fabric.

Suddenly, Shady Elf is behind me, his warm breath tickling my ear as he pours more whiskey all over my ass and lower back. It's like it's his signature move, or he just really likes whiskey, but again, either way I'm not complaining. He traces it slowly with his tongue, tasting the amber liquid as it glistens on my skin. I shudder at the heat he creates, my pussy clenching around Mr. Claus' fingers.

"That's it," he murmurs against my skin, licking a hot trail down to where our bodies meet and nudging Mr. Claus out of the way. I feel Shady swirl his tongue around my entrance teasingly, and then he dives in, lapping at my pussy from behind like a starving creature.

The sensations are too much and I writhe under his touch, bucking my hips up into his face. I hear Sultry Elf laugh softly, and then she's gone, presumably to find another victim for our game.

"But what about me?" Demanding Elf asks, puffing out his chest proudly in that custom-made suit with the perfectly placed pocket square.

"You can join when you find someone of your own," Sultry Elf calls back over her shoulder, her curls bouncing playfully as she disappears around a corner.

Shady Elf continues to lap at me, his long talented tongue tracing patterns on my sensitive flesh that make me moan uncontrollably. As he laps up every last drop of his whiskey from my cunt, I feel myself getting closer to the edge.

"Fuck," I mutter, grabbing onto the counter for leverage as another wave of pleasure washes over me. I've missed this—the taste of myself on a man's tongue, the feel of his mouth exploring every inch of me. "Oh fuck, Shady Elf."

He pulls away slowly, chuckling darkly. "Do you want more?" He asks with a glint in his eye.

I nod eagerly, my eyes fluttering shut as he applies more of the sharp liquid to my entrance. This time, however, he pushes inside me, filling me up with his velvet cock. It's rough but so incredibly good, it's almost painful how much I need this.

My husband groans at the site of another man's cock impaling my pussy.

"Oh God!" I cry out, arching my back and meeting his thrusts with my own. My moans fill the otherwise silent kitchen, and I can't help but wish we could stay like this forever—but I know it's always going to be quick and dirty when we're together.

Just as I'm about to come apart in his arms, he pulls out and hits his cock against my clit before groaning and pulsing inside me.

"Merry fucking Christmas," he whispers hoarsely.

I lean down to catch my breath, watching as he licks the last drops of whiskey off his fingers. "That was...fucking amazing," I manage to get out between pants.

"Thank you," he replies smugly, grabbing my ass and pulling me closer for another deep kiss.

I can't help but smile against his lips, my heart racing. "You're always welcome," I murmur as I kiss him again.

We break apart, both panting heavily, and look over to see Demanding Elf and Sultry Elf standing there, their eyes sparkling with mischief.

"The two of you spend so much time giggling," Demanding Elf says, seemingly nonchalant but clearly turned on. "We thought we should come by and see what all the fun was about."

Shady Elf smirks. "We still have some things to teach you two, don't we?"

I can't help but feel a shiver run down my spine at the thought of what they might have in store for us. Their eyes are dark with lust, their bodies practically vibrating with anticipation.

I roll my eyes but laugh. "Sure, come on in then."

They both grin and approach us, looking like they're about to pounce. Demanding Elf has a wicked glint in his eye as he runs his hand up my leg teasingly, while Sultry Elf bites her bottom lip suggestively. "We thought you might need some...more"—he pauses dramatically—"entertainment."

Mr. Claus chuckles. "We most certainly couldn't refuse such an offer. Didn't I do a good job with my suggestion, honey?"

The six of us lock eyes, and without another word, they all move towards us on the bed, our nerves tingling with excitement. They climb onto the bed, Demanding Elf sitting on the edge while Sultry Elf crawls under the covers with us. I can't help but feel a sense of awe as they take control. Their confidence is both sexy and reassuring.

Demanding Elf unbuttons his shirt slowly, revealing his chiseled torso and eager cock straining against his pants. Shady Elf does the same thing on the other side of me. It's a show of dominance that makes my heart race even faster.

Sultry Elf crawls between us, licking her plump lips suggestively as she watches us undress. She groans softly as she sees my naked body, her gaze lingering on my breasts before meeting my eyes. "You look delicious," she says, that smoky voice sending shivers down my spine.

Finally, we're all naked—except for our stockings and collars—and it's like Christmas came early for these sexy elves as they begin to explore every inch of us. Their tongues dance across our skin like snowflakes on a windowpane, their fingers tugging gently at our nipples and teasing our clits. My husband looks over me as hands ravish his cuddly body. It's a sensory overload: soft fur from the bedspread, hard abs, wild whispers, and hot breaths.

It becomes an erotic dance, filled with moans and gasps, our bodies moving together in perfect harmony as we create a symphony of passion under the twinkling lights of the tree.

Shady Elf's whiskey-soaked tongue dances over my pussy lips, tracing gentle circles around my clit before plunging inside. I gasp as he pushes further, tasting my sweet nectar mixed with his whiskey. His beard scrapes against my skin, sending shivers down my spine.

Demanding Elf watches with a mix of lust and curiosity from the corner of the bed, licking his lips. Sultry Elf's large breasts heave with every breath.

"Mmm, you all look so good together," she murmurs, her voice like velvet, "I can't help but join in on this fun." She kneels beside me, her breath hot against my ear as she speaks. Before I can react, she takes Shady Elf's place, her tongue now lapping at my juices. Her touch is rougher than his, but no less electrifying. As she works her magic, my body shudders uncontrollably under their dual assault.

Shady Elf's fingers trace my body, dipping into the pool of desire Sultry Elf is creating, mixing our fluids together. Demanding Elf's eyes glint with desire as he watches his whiskey-soaked finger disappear into me, his tongue circling my clit.

"Fuck," I moan, unable to contain myself any longer. "This is too much."

"That's it, baby," Sultry Elf murmurs, her voice low and sultry like her name suggests, "let go."

And just like that, I do. Waves of pleasure crash over me, washing away every thought but their touch and taste. I feel them both drinking me in greedily, marking me as theirs. When I finally come, it's explosive–my whole body shaking uncontrollably under their ministrations.

My husband, eyes dark with lust, helps me up, pulling me into a passionate kiss that leaves me dizzy. "You elves are incredible," he pants, "But remember, you're still mine, Mrs. Claus."

I smile against his lips, feeling the rough stubble on his cheek tickling my skin. "And you're mine, Mr. Claus," I whisper back, our eyes meeting in a heated exchange of promises and secrets.

As we disentangle ourselves from each other, the six of us catch our breaths together. We lick our lips, tasting the remnants of each other on them like a potent aphrodisiac.

Our gazes locked on one another's bodies, we share a loaded moment before going back to our work–making toys for all the good girls and boys around the world and preparing to deliver them house by house. The scent of freshly cut wood mingling with sweat and desire, filling the air of the usually sterile workshop.

The jingling of bells on the door startles us all, but it's just a group of reindeer bringing a list of even more gifts for us to make. We laugh together, high on the sultry heat that still lingers between us as if it were mistletoe.

The day continues with an undercurrent of desire pulsating beneath the surface. Every glance, every touch, every conversation holds a new meaning now that we've crossed this line. We finish up late into the night, our hands working almost unconsciously to create the perfect gifts for children everywhere while our minds are still very much on each other.

Finally, the last gift is made, and Shady Elf and I stand up wearily. Sultry Elf watches us, her eyes gleaming with unspoken fantasies.

"Well then," Demanding Elf says, clapping his hands together, "it's time for milk and cookies. Santa will be home at any moment." He turns to me. "Are you ready, my dear?"

I nod eagerly, my stomach growling in anticipation. Tonight's feast will be different—sweeter, naughtier. We all know it.

We head into the living room, a fire crackling in the hearth, stockings hung by the chimney with care still filled with goodies from earlier. Demanding Elf helps me onto the couch, his large hands cupping my ass gently as he sits down beside me. He pulls me close, our bare skin pressed together like magnets.

"Now," he murmurs in my ear, "how about some dessert first?"

He lifts a pint of whiskey, uncorks it and pours some onto his hand before tracing it down my neck, over my collarbone, teasing my breasts until it drips onto the valley between them. He brings his lips to my nipple, lapping up the alcohol while his fingers find their way into my panties, rubbing teasingly against my clit.

Sultry Elf moves closer to us, running her fingers through Shady Elf's hair as she watches our intimate exchange.

"Let me help you," she purrs, taking the bottle from Demanding Elf and pouring some over her own hand. She smells like vanilla and spice, intoxicating and sweet on the tip of my tongue.

She begins to trail fire-warmed whiskey over my other breast and down my stomach, stopping to dip her fingers into my panties just like Demanding Elf did before. Her touch is soft yet demanding, making me shiver with anticipation.

Shady Elf watches as Sultry Elf licks the whiskey from my stomach, her tongue dancing over me like a flame. "You're so fucking sexy tonight," she whispers, tracing the lines of my abs with her finger before bringing it to her mouth for a taste.

Their scent fills my head, making me dizzy with arousal.

Sultry Elf moves down between my legs, her fingers sliding my wetness over her lips as she tastes me, savoring every drop. Then she looks up at us with a sly grin. "What do you think?" She asks, one eyebrow raised.

Demanding Elf doesn't hesitate to answer, pulling me into a deep kiss while Shady Elf whispers, "I like it."

We curl into each other, our lovemaking fueled by their presence. As we reach our climax, we can feel the fireplace grow hotter, the room darker–and then we see them blinking into existence before us: hot chocolate, soft fuzzy socks, and an ornament falling to the ground. It's Christmas morning.

A moment later, Mr. Claus enters the room. He looks tired but seems to perk up at the sight of Sultry lapping at my pussy like a starving woman.

"Well, then..." he says, "I thought I'd take a shower and then a nap when I got home, but now I think I'm going to skip the nap part. There are clearly far more important things to attend to..."

The Babysitter Brings a Friend(FFFM)

Unintended Playthings(FFMM)

Hot Girl Summer: The Ice Cream Shop(FM)

A Weekend with my Girlfriends (Audio) (FFFFFF)

Stack of Pleasure(FFFFFM)

Dinner for Three(MFM)

Ordering In(MMF)

Inviting the Babysitter(FFM)

Jenny Asks to Join(FFFM)

Reverse(FMMMM)

Recipe for Seduction(FFM)

Getting Freaky at the Tiki(FFM)
Collections:

Very Sexy Bedtime Stories

Neighborhood Playthings Collection: A Trio of Very Sexy Erotic Stories

The Adventures Collection

The Arrangements Collection: A Satisfying Trio of Sexy Stories

The Hot Girl Summer Collection: A Trio of Sexy Stories
See the rest at https://www.amazon.com/author/mcplains